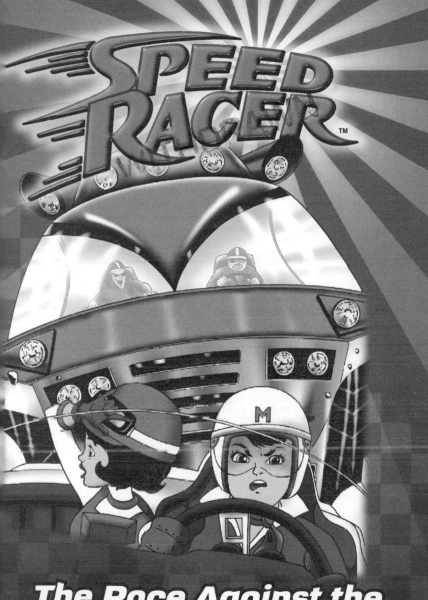

The Race Against the

Mammoth Car

GROSSET & DUNLAP
Published by the Penguin Group
Penguin Group (USA) Inc., 375 Hudson Street,
New York, New York 10014, USA
Penguin Group (Canada), 90 Eglinton Avenue East,
Suite 700, Toronto, Ontario M4P 2Y3, Canada
(a division of Pearson Penguin Canada Inc.)
Penguin Books Ltd., 80 Strand, London WC2R 0RL, England
Penguin Group Ireland, 25 St. Stephen's Green, Dublin 2, Ireland
(a division of Penguin Books Ltd.)
Penguin Group (Australia), 250 Camberwell Road,
Camberwell, Victoria 3124, Australia
(a division of Pearson Australia Group Pty. Ltd.)
Penguin Books India Pvt. Ltd., 11 Community Centre,
Panchsheel Park, New Delhi—110 017, India
Penguin Group (NZ), 67 Apollo Drive, Rosedale,
North Shore 0632, New Zealand
(a division of Pearson New Zealand Ltd.)
Penguin Books (South Africa) (Pty.) Ltd., 24 Sturdee Avenue,
Rosebank, Johannesburg 2196, South Africa

Penguin Books Ltd., Registered Offices:
80 Strand, London WC2R 0RL, England

www.speedracer.com

Designed by Michelle Martinez Design, Inc.

Library of Congress Cataloging-in-Publication Data is available.

ISBN 978-0-448-44807-7   10 9 8 7 6 5 4 3 2 1

SPEED RACER ™

The Race Against the

Mammoth Car

by Chase Wheeler   Grosset & Dunlap

The Marvels of the Mach 5

The Mach 5 is one of the most
powerful and amazing racing cars in
the world. Pops Racer designed the Mach 5
with features you won't see on any other car.
All of the features can be controlled by
buttons on the steering wheel.

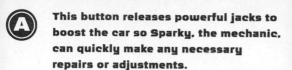

A This button releases powerful jacks to boost the car so Sparky. the mechanic, can quickly make any necessary repairs or adjustments.

B Press this button and the Mach 5 sprouts special grip tires for traction over any terrain. At the same time, an incredible 5,000 torque of horsepower is distributed equally to each wheel by auxiliary engines.

C For use when Speed Racer has to race over heavily wooded terrain, powerful rotary saws protrude from the front of the Mach 5 to slash and cut any and all obstacles.

D Pressing the D button releases a powerful deflector that seals the cockpit into an air-conditioned, crash and bulletproof, watertight chamber. Inside it, Speed Racer is completely isolated and shielded.

E The button for special illumination allows Speed Racer to see much farther and more clearly than with ordinary headlights. It's invaluable in some of the weird and dangerous places he races the Mach 5.

F Press this button when the Mach 5 is underwater. First the cockpit is supplied with oxygen, then a periscope is raised to scan the surface of the water. Everything that is seen is relayed down to the cockpit by television.

G This releases a homing robot from the front of the car. The homing robot can carry pictures or tape-recorded messages to anyone or anywhere Speed Racer wants.

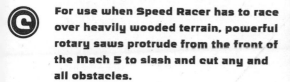

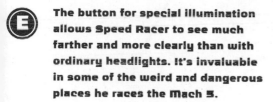

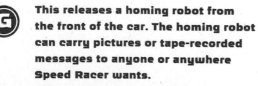

Speed Racer, driver for the Go Team, sat ready in his race car: the incredible, incomparable Mach 5. Speed was at the starting point of the five-hundred-mile No-Limit World Race, a race that would take the drivers offtrack and onto real roads. The race would wind through deserts and up mountains and past oceans, ending outside the country. It was billed as the longest car race in the world.

Speed and the other racers were in a huge stadium packed with thousands of cheering spectators. The Mach 5 was lifted many feet off the ground atop its hydraulic jack so the Go Team's top mechanic, Sparky, could make some last-minute adjustments.

"Okay, Speed!" Sparky shouted from beneath the car. "The brakes and the wheel systems are in perfect condition. We're all set. Let's get ready to race."

"Watch out, Sparky!" Speed called. He disengaged the jack, and the Mach 5's tires lowered to the ground with a smooth, solid bounce. He was about to pull into position when he heard someone calling his name.

"Speed! Wait, Speed! Wait for me!" It was Trixie, a key member of the Go Team and Speed's girlfriend. She was running madly across the track dressed in her red racing uniform and matching helmet.

Sparky was just about to get into the Mach

5 when Trixie leaped past him. She hopped into the Mach 5's passenger seat and shut the door in Sparky's face. Since the No-Limit World Race was so long, drivers were able to take along assistant drivers as backups—and to help if there were any mechanical problems along the way. But the Mach 5 could only hold one assistant driver. Obviously, Trixie thought she was the one going on the race with Speed.

Sparky stood outside the car, dazed. He had assumed he'd be Speed's assistant driver.

"You know you won't win if you don't have me for your assistant," Trixie said to Speed. Then she winked.

Trixie and Sparky weren't the only members of the Go Team who expected to come along for the race. Speed's little brother, Spritle, and his pet chimpanzee, Chim Chim, popped open the trunk of the Mach 5. Since the Mach 5 was designed as a two-seat race car, its trunk was where Spritle and Chim Chim were used to traveling. They liked to sneak in whenever they could.

"Hop in, Chim Chim," Spritle said. He helped Chim Chim into the trunk and jumped in after him.

But before they got the trunk closed, their father, Pops Racer, reached in and pulled them both out.

"Spritle, you know there's no room for you in the Mach 5 during a race. I built this car to hold only two people," Pops said firmly. "We can't have anything—or anyone—slowing down the Mach 5 during this big race."

Racing cars ran in the Racer family. Pops was the head of the Go Team and an extremely

talented race car designer. The Mach 5 was his greatest design, and he was very proud to have his son Speed be the one to drive it. Pops had another, older son—Rex—who long ago wanted to become a professional race car driver, but Pops had been too worried about his safety to let that happen. Rex wouldn't give up on his dream, so he had run away from home years ago. The family hadn't seen Rex since.

Now, Pops's second son, Speed, had the same dream to become a professional race car driver. Even though Pops was often worried about his safety, he tried to be as supportive as possible. He saw how much racing cars meant to Speed. And Pops didn't want to risk losing another son.

"You ready for the big race, Speed?" Pops called. He closed the trunk securely so Spritle and Chim Chim couldn't sneak back in.

"Almost," Speed said. "I just need an assistant driver."

He was looking back and forth between

Trixie and Sparky, who were now in a full-blown argument about who would be his assistant.

"Trixie," Sparky was saying, "I know every single part of the Mach 5. You know I'm the best mechanic. Just let me ride in the race with Speed."

"Oh?" Trixie said, raising an eyebrow. She wouldn't budge from the passenger seat. "I know every part of the car just as well as you do, Sparky. And I can do everything for the Mach 5 that you can do." It was true that Trixie was a skilled mechanic. Every member of the Go Team—except maybe Chim Chim—had serious skill with cars.

"But this is the most important race the team's ever been in," Sparky pleaded. "Please let me ride."

Trixie crossed her arms defiantly. "No way," she said. "I'm the assistant."

"Get out of the car!" Sparky shouted.

"Never!" Trixie shouted right back.

Speed had had enough of their bickering. He had made his decision.

"Sparky, just let it go. Let Trixie ride with me this time," he said. Then he looked out toward the starting point on the racetrack. "See? No time to argue. The other cars are getting into position."

The Go Team forgot the disagreement as they looked out at all the different cars pulling up to the starting line. There were cars of every model and make. Classic cars. Brand-new cars. Specially designed cars. Exotic cars that no one had ever seen before. Cars in every color, size, and shape.

"Wow!" Sparky said, forgetting his anger. "Look at those cars. This should be some amazing race. Any kind of car can enter!"

"That's right," Trixie said. "Any kind of car is allowed in this race. There are cars from all over the world."

"So that means all kinds of drivers," Sparky said. "You can't know what to expect, Speed. It could be dangerous."

Speed took it all in. He was confident that the Mach 5 could beat every car on this track. He just had to drive his best to make it happen.

All of a sudden, everyone gasped in unison as a gigantic car barreled onto the race track.

Black smoke curled from its exhaust pipes and

its engine roared like a raging monster.

"Hey, look at that!" someone in the crowd shouted.

"That's the biggest car I've ever seen!" someone else shouted.

The gigantic car was as tall as a house. It was dark red, with a huge grille in front that made it look like it had a nasty, snarling mouth. The car was made of eleven connected segments, making it hundreds of feet longer than any other car in the race. The only windows were in the front, like two bright, angry eyes. In fact, the gigantic car looked more like a train than a regular car. As it pulled into position at the starting line, the crowd went silent. This car dwarfed every other car on the track.

"That car's almost as long as a football field," Sparky said in disbelief.

Speed shook his head in wonder. With Trixie sitting at his side, he pulled the Mach 5 into position.

Once all the cars were in place, an announcement came over the stadium's loudspeaker:

"Hello, racing fans. The officials will now inspect the cars in the great No-Limit World Race!" The crowd yelled impatiently for the race to start.

The officials made their way over to the Mach 5.

"Time to inspect your car, Speed," the lead official said.

Sparky ran over. "I have a question," he said. "The rules say that any kind of car can be in the race, so why do you have to bother inspecting them?"

"There's a good reason, Sparky," answered Inspector Detector as he approached the Mach 5.

"Oh, Inspector Detector. We didn't know you'd be at the big race," Sparky said.

"How are you, Inspector?" Speed asked. He reached out to shake the detective's hand. Speed often found himself involved in Inspector Detector's police investigations. Inspector Detector

was always trying to find a way to help keep the bad guys off the streets.

"Oh, I'm all right, Speed," Inspector Detector replied with a smile. "Glad to see you here. But that's not the reason I came to the track today." His face turned serious. "Fifty million dollars in gold bars were stolen from the National Bank last week."

"Yes, I remember reading about that, sir," Speed said.

"Well," the detective began, lowering his voice, "it's possible that someone might try to smuggle those gold bars out of the country some time during this race. This is our only chance to search the cars. We can't afford to let the robbers get away with a fortune like that!"

"But fifty million dollars in gold bars . . ." Trixie burst in. "That's a lot of gold! It would take an awfully big car to smuggle it away in, wouldn't it?"

"Yes, it certainly would," Inspector Detector agreed. "But the bank robbers were very clever. We think we know who they're working for, but we still haven't been able to find the gold. We think they might have found a way to make the gold bars smaller. Or they could have hidden the gold bars inside a car somehow. We're open to any possibility. So we even have to inspect your car, Speed."

Speed nodded to show that he didn't mind.

The officials opened the hood of the Mach 5 and began searching around.

"So, who do you think the bank robbers are working for?" Speed asked.

"Have you ever heard of Cruncher Block?" Inspector Detector said.

"Oh, sure," Speed said. "He's one of the richest men in the world."

"We're sure he's the head of the robbers, and we know he'd stop at nothing to get that gold out of the country."

After a few minutes of thorough checking, the lead official gave Inspector Detector a thumbs-up. "The Mach 5 passes inspection, Inspector," the official said.

"Good. Well, good luck, Go Team," Inspector Detector said.

"Thanks!" Speed said.

Inspector Detector and the racing officials moved to the Mammoth Car to continue their inspection. It certainly was a car big enough to hold that much gold. With all those compartments, there was definitely enough room to hide it.

The Mammoth Car's driver leaned out of the window far up above the ground. He had a nasty face and a big, loud mouth. "You go right ahead," he yelled at the racing officials. "Look around all you want. You ain't gonna find nothin'."

"This car looks too big for the race," Inspector Detector said. "It doesn't seem fair to me."

"It is fair!" one of the Mammoth Car's driving assistants yelled. "The rules say any kind of car can enter. This is a car. It's just a really long car."

Because the Mammoth Car was so big, it had many driving assistants. Speed had just one assistant driver for the race, but the Mammoth Car had at least ten.

Another assistant yelled down to Inspector Detector. "Hey, you. You want a tour of the Mammoth Car? Then come on up."

Inspector Detector climbed the tall steps and entered the first compartment of the enormous vehicle.

"The main engine has seventy-five hundred horsepower," the Mammoth Car's assistant driver told him. "Each mammoth wheel also contains an

individual engine of fifteen hundred horsepower. Altogether, the Mammoth Car is driven by thirty thousand horsepower." He began to walk Inspector Detector and the racing officials through the huge interior. Each compartment was just a giant, empty room.

"Hmm," was all the detective said as he looked around. So far, there were no gold bars in sight.

Outside the Mammoth Car, Sparky was doing some inspecting of his own. As an auto mechanic, he was always curious about cars. And he'd never

seen such a massive vehicle in his entire life. His curiosity got the better of him. He walked the entire length of the Mammoth Car to get a closer look.

◎   ◎   ◎   ◎

Back inside the Mammoth Car, an assistant driver continued giving a tour to Inspector Detector and the racing officials.

"The Mammoth Car can travel over five hundred miles per hour on any kind of road," the Mammoth Car's driver bragged in a loud, booming voice. "The brakes are magnetic and a single push of a button will stop the car. We have an army of mechanics that can fix anything if something goes wrong."

The Mammoth Car's driver walked Inspector Detector and the racing officials all the way to the very last compartment of the car. Every compartment they passed through was as empty as the first. There were no gold bars. No boxes holding gold bars. It appeared to hide nothing.

The driver showed Inspector Detector and the racing officials to the sliding metal door in the back of the Mammoth Car. He opened it, and they climbed down to the ground.

"This car is so powerful, we can't possibly lose this race," the Mammoth Car's driver announced. Then he waved and closed the door.

Sparky, who had been peering closely at the Mammoth Car's giant taillights, approached Inspector Detector.

"Did you find out how many cylinders the engine has and if it's equipped with a supercharger?" he asked excitedly.

"That car's equipped with anything anybody could imagine," said Inspector Detector with a sigh.

"Oh," Sparky said. His face fell when he realized that a car like this would be very hard to beat. Even for the Mach 5.

As Inspector Detector and the racing officials walked away to inspect another car, Sparky snuck a peek at the underside of the Mammoth Car. Curious, he crawled underneath the Mammoth Car and began poking around.

When he crawled out, he was met by the car's lead driver. The driver stood there menacingly, a large wrench held tightly in his fist.

"Spying on us, are you?" he growled.

"I was just trying to find out if your car was equipped with any special inventions I didn't know about," Sparky said. "I just like to know—"

"You want to know all about the Mammoth

Car, eh?" the driver snapped. "Okay. I'll be glad to show you around. But let's take a little detour first. Come on." He grabbed Sparky by the collar and dragged him across the track.

"Aaaah! Help!" Sparky shouted.

But with the noise of the crowd and the roar of so many engines, no one heard him.

The Mammoth Car's driver dragged Sparky to an empty storage area where no one in the stadium could see them. He shoved Sparky inside and punched him in the face, knocking him flat on his back. Then the driver stepped outside, made sure the door was locked, and closed it with a sinister laugh. Sparky was trapped inside.

All the car inspections were over, and the five-hundred-mile No-Limit World Race was about to begin.

Pops, Spritle, and Chim Chim gathered around the Mach 5. Speed and Trixie were in the car. But someone was missing.

"Where's Sparky?" Speed asked. "He's not still mad about Trixie being my assistant, is he?"

"No, not at all," Pops said. "But I don't see him around anywhere." He put a hand over his eyes and scanned the stadium. Sparky was nowhere to be seen.

"He might be up to mischief!" Spritle shrieked. "I know I would be if I were him, right?"

"Right, Spritle. But you're not Sparky," Trixie said.

"The race is about to begin. Start your

engines!" the announcer called out over the stadium's loudspeaker.

Wherever Sparky was, they'd have to find out later.

"Here goes," Speed said. He lowered his racing visor and started the engine.

Looking across the track, Trixie noticed someone watching them.

"Who's that?" Trixie asked.

"Huh?" Speed said. He was unable to make out who was watching them through the thick cloud of engine exhaust and the crowd of spectators.

Had he been able to see, he would have realized that the person watching them was the famous masked driver, Racer X. Unknown to Speed, Racer X was actually his older brother, Rex. Racer X kept an eye out for Speed. He was always around to protect him, even if Speed didn't know it.

"Ready . . ." the announcer began. Engines revved. "Set . . ." the announcer continued. "Go!" Tires squealed.

The race had begun! The sound of a great many engines roared through the stadium.

Right away, the enormous Mammoth Car took the lead. But soon enough, much to the crowd's delight, Speed raced the Mach 5 right past it to take the top position. Pops, Spritle, and Chim Chim cheered for Speed as the Mach 5 zipped over the racetrack in a flash of bright white.

In the stands, a mean-looking man in a gleaming white suit grinned to himself. His eyes were on one car and one car only: the Mammoth Car. His Mammoth Car.

After a quick lap around the track, the drivers exited the stadium and headed onto the main highway.

◉　　◉　　◉　　◉

Sparky lay semiconscious on the floor of the storage room.

"Come on, Sparky, get up," a voice said.

Sparky slowly opened his eyes. He rubbed his head. Standing over him was none other than Racer X.

"You…look…familiar," Sparky mumbled. One of his eyes was swelling up. He was sure to get a black eye.

"Tell me what happened," Racer X said. He helped Sparky to his feet.

"I was looking at the Mammoth Car when the driver grabbed me, dragged me in here, and knocked me out," Sparky explained.

"The Mammoth Car's driver, huh?" Racer X said. He suddenly seemed very concerned.

Back in the race, the drivers had gone a good distance past the city and were now moving through the less-populated, mountainous area of the race. Suddenly, the Mammoth Car was being driven more aggressively. With no racing officials nearby to see, the Mammoth Car's driver threw out the rule book. He began running the other cars off the road.

One by one, the Mammoth Car rammed into and knocked out every other car on the road. The cars were hurtled into rock walls, run off cliffs, or forced to lose tires and spin out. In minutes, only the Mammoth Car and the Mach 5 were left in the race.

Speed stepped down hard on the Mach 5's accelerator to pull farther into the lead and, more importantly, to create some distance between it and the dangerous Mammoth Car. He took the Mach 5 to top speed.

But no matter how fast Speed was driving, it was still no match for the massive amount of horsepower in the Mammoth Car.

In the blink of an eye, the Mammoth Car closed the distance between it and the Mach 5.

Trixie screamed. The Mammoth Car was behind the Mach 5. It was about to ram right into them!

Realizing that he couldn't outpace the Mammoth Car, Speed pressed the B button on the Mach 5's steering-wheel control panel. Pops had

designed the Mach 5 with special features that made it much more than an ordinary race car. The B button engaged the grip tires, giving the Mach 5 extra traction on even the most difficult terrain.

Just as the Mammoth Car was about to slam into the Mach 5, Speed turned the steering wheel hard. He veered off the highway and up onto the side of the mountain. The belt tires clung to the rocky mountainside, allowing him to drive out of harm's way.

The Mammoth Car barreled forward, taking the lead on the road below.

Having safely avoided the collision, Speed maneuvered the Mach 5 back onto the road. He kept close behind the Mammoth Car, his eyes on it at all times.

A short distance ahead, a red signal was flashing at the railroad crossing. A freight train was approaching on the tracks. They would have to stop the race and let it go by.

The Mammoth Car ignored the signal and

sped right across the railroad tracks.

The freight train tooted its whistle, but it was too late. The Mammoth Car was far too long to cross the tracks in one quick shot. The engineer hit the brake, but the massively long Mammoth Car was still in the way. The train couldn't stop quickly enough. It smashed headfirst into the last section of the Mammoth Car. There was a loud crash as the train broke into pieces from the impact and flew off the track, completely demolished from the collision.

The Mammoth Car, shockingly, was barely damaged. Still, it slowed to a stop.

Speed had stopped the Mach 5 beside the

tracks. He and Trixie had their hands over their mouths in shock.

As the dust settled, they saw the train crew climbing out of the wreckage.

"Come on," Speed said. "Let's go see if anyone's been hurt."

While Speed and Trixie helped the train's crew, the Mammoth Car's mechanics quickly dealt with the minor scratches from the accident. The Mammoth Car had barely anything to fix. All the team of mechanics had to do was repaint the exterior in a few spots.

After spraying the scratched areas with a thin coat of red paint, the mechanics filed back inside the Mammoth Car. They didn't even glance at the wrecked train to see if they could help. The Mammoth Car's engine started up with a booming growl and a burst of dark smoke. Then the massive vehicle pulled away and returned to the race.

"The Mammoth Car's leaving! Let's go!" Speed cried.

Speed and Trixie checked one last time to make sure that the train's crew was okay, and then they jumped into the Mach 5 and took off after the Mammoth Car.

Back on the highway, Speed followed the Mammoth Car at a safe distance.

"That's very weird," Speed said. "The Mammoth Car was hardly scratched in the crash, so why did the mechanics rush out to repair it like that? Trixie, I'll bet there's some kind of mysterious secret to the whole thing."

"A secret?" Trixie said. "I wonder what it could be."

"Let's use the homing robot to find out," Speed suggested.

Trixie nodded. "We can attach a camera to the homing robot and then send it over to the Mammoth Car without them knowing! I'll set the camera to take X-ray photographs. That way, we'll be able to see straight through the Mammoth Car's metal exterior to what's inside!"

"There has to be some kind of secret cargo inside, something Inspector Detector missed," Speed said. "Why else would they need a car that big?"

Trixie opened a compartment on the dashboard and removed a miniscule high-tech camera. She made a quick adjustment to the camera, setting it to take X-ray images. Then she secured the camera to the Mach 5's homing robot.

"The homing robot's all ready for flight, Speed. If anything can tell us what the Mammoth Car is

carrying, this sure will," Trixie said.

Using the homing robot's remote control, Speed launched the camera-equipped device into the air. At first the homing robot flew beside the Mammoth Car, its X-ray camera trained on the walls of each of its long segments. But then one of the members of the Mammoth Car's driving crew happened to glance out the window and saw it hovering there. The homing robot was designed to look like a pigeon. But what kind of pigeon could fly that fast?

Suspicious, the crew member looked out the window.

That was no living pigeon—it was a tiny robot designed to look like a pigeon!

The crew member knocked the robot in the head, swatting it away from the Mammoth Car. The homing robot started to wobble, losing momentum. The Mammoth Car took off, leaving the homing robot in its dust.

From behind them on the road, Speed and Trixie saw that something had happened to the homing robot. "Signal the robot back!" Trixie cried.

Speed hit the return button, and the homing robot crookedly flew back to the Mach 5. Speed kept driving, staying on the Mammoth Car's tail. The homing robot landed with a thump in Trixie's hands.

"Oh no," she said. "Somebody hit it." The crew member had smashed the camera. Whatever X-ray pictures it had taken were lost forever.

On the road ahead, the Mammoth Car held its lead. While staying on course, it sent a radio signal to a mansion hidden away in the hills.

This was the luxurious secret headquarters of the Mammoth Car's owner: the notorious Cruncher Block.

Cruncher Block was a thick, loud man well used to getting his way. He was one of the richest men in the world, and he wanted to get even richer. He lounged out in the sunshine, wearing a spiffy white suit, waiting for word from the Mammoth Car. When the radio signal came through, he bolted up in his lounge chair.

The Mammoth Car's driver reported the news.

"Speed Racer sent a flying robot camera to spy on us?!" Cruncher Block bellowed. "We'd better get rid of them. Now, you listen to me. You've gotta stay in the race, no matter what that kid throws at you."

"Yes, sir," the driver said.

Cruncher Block kept bellowing. "The only way

to get the fifty million bucks in gold bars outta the country is if you stay in this race. That way, you'll get over the border with no trouble. You hear me?"

Cruncher Block disconnected the radio without waiting for an answer. Then he spit on the ground and looked up into the bright sun. He knew his Mammoth Car would get his loot out of the country. It had to. It was the only way.

The Mammoth Car kept driving in the long No-Limit World Race. The sun was setting in the sky, but the race was still going. They forged ahead, crossing mountains and rivers, getting closer to the country's border with every passing mile.

But at the Mammoth Car's back was always the white race car: the Mach 5.

In the Mach 5, Trixie glanced in the rearview mirror and noticed that there were no other cars on the road behind them. No headlights could be seen in the distance.

"I don't see any other cars, Speed," she said.

"Now the race is just between us and the Mammoth Car," Speed said, wiping some sweat from his brow.

Trixie nodded.

"But I still think there's something not right

with the Mammoth Car," Speed said. "Why else would they have knocked the homing robot out like that? They must be carrying the gold."

"I think you're right, Speed," Trixie said. "But how can we be sure?"

"I'm going up there," Speed said.

He shifted gears, and the Mach 5 burst ahead on the road. He switched lanes so the Mach 5 was driving beside the Mammoth Car, keeping pace with the enormous vehicle. He drove past the tail segment and past several others. The Mammoth Car was as long as a train, with dozens of tires that were twice the height of the Mach 5.

As Speed drove beside the Mammoth Car, Trixie looked out the side window, studying the huge spinning tires. She had to crane her neck to see up any higher than that.

Seeing the Mach 5's daring approach, the Mammoth Car let out a blast of dark smoke from exhaust pipes near the tire axles. The smoke blinded Speed for a moment, but it was a moment

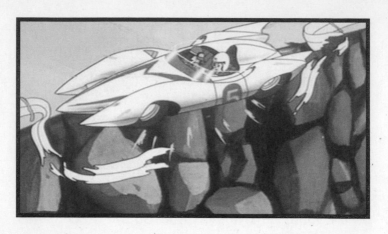

long enough for the Mammoth Car to force the Mach 5 in the wrong direction. Just as they were approaching a swift turn on a mountainside, the Mammoth Car gave the Mach 5 a shove. The Mach 5 spun out of control, hitting the guardrail and careening off the road.

The Mach 5 fell a few feet, landing on an outcropping of rocks. The Mammoth Car kept going as if nothing had happened.

Trixie gasped.

"Hang on!" Speed yelled. He pushed a button on the Mach 5's steering column to activate the belt tires. But the belt tires spun and spun in the loose gravel and rock, unable to get enough traction to take off.

"Speed, look!" Trixie yelled.

It wasn't enough that the Mach 5 was stuck on the side of the road—not for the Mammoth Car. They had to make sure that Speed Racer was out of this race for good.

One of the Mammoth Car's many compartments came open, and a ramp slid down to the surface of the road. Motorcycles started pouring out.

There were too many motorcycles, speeding too quickly, for Speed or Trixie to count. They had bright headlights on in the dark. That's all that Speed and Trixie could see from their spot in the rocks: a great many bright lights heading straight at them.

Speed kept gunning the engine, trying to give the belt tires enough traction to take off and get the Mach 5 back on the road.

Would the belt tires take hold? Would the

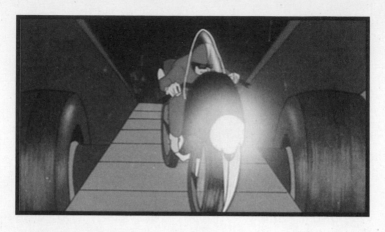

motorcycles get to him first?

There was no time to think. Speed had no idea what to do.

But someone did.

Suddenly, Speed spied a yellow streak on the road.

"Another car!" he cried.

It was Racer X, appearing on the road in his trademark yellow race car. He must have been monitoring the race from the shadows.

Racer X sprayed oil all over the road, which was not visible in the nighttime, and the motorcyclists drove straight onto it without realizing. They spun out of control. One motorcycle hit a patch of the oil and keeled over. Another hit the oil slick and slammed straight into a rock wall. Another driver flew off his motorcycle completely and did a wild flying leap into another driver, knocking him off his motorcycle, too.

Thanks to Racer X, all of the motorcycles were out of commission.

Just in time, too, because that's when the Mach 5's belt tires finally got a good grip in the gravel and took off. Speed was back in the race. The Mammoth Car had gotten a good lead, but Speed knew he could catch it.

"Thanks to Racer X, we can go on now," Trixie said. "Go!"

Speed narrowed his eyes on the road ahead. The Mach 5 was back on the road, back in the race, and back in pursuit of the Mammoth Car.

Far away from the last two cars in the No-Limit World Race, Pops Racer was driving his own car on another road. The top was down, and he was speeding through the night with a look of serious determination. Sitting in the passenger seat was the Mach 5's dedicated mechanic, Sparky. He still looked dazed from his confrontation with the Mammoth Car's driver. He'd just told Pops everything he knew about the Mammoth Car. He was sure that something fishy was going on.

"I see," Pops said, keeping his foot steady on the gas as they whipped down the road. "So the driver of the Mammoth Car slugged you, huh? It's clear they'll stop at nothing to win this race. There's no way we'll catch up to Speed now. So we've got to take a plane to where they are and try to help them."

"Is that where you're taking us, Pops?" Sparky said. He was still not feeling 100 percent. His eye had swollen up to a good shiner.

"That's right, Sparky," Pops said into the wind. "We're going to the airport."

By the time Pops and Sparky reached the closest airport, they were the last customers at the airline counter. Through the window, in the dark night sky, they could see a plane taking off on the runway.

"What do you mean that was the last plane leaving for the north tonight?" Pops cried to the airline employee. "I don't believe it! We've got to fly there."

The airline attendant smiled blandly, not caring that Pops had missed the plane.

"Well," the airline attendant said, "unless you can sprout wings and fly north yourself, you'll just have to wait. The next plane leaves at seven tomorrow morning."

"Seven!" Pops cried. "But my son Speed Racer is in the north. He's in the big race. And he may need our help. Are you sure there isn't an earlier plane?"

As Pops argued with the airline attendant, there was something going on in Pops's car parked just outside.

The trunk came open and out popped two small heads.

It was Spritle and Chim Chim. They'd stowed away in Pops's car!

Spritle and Chim Chim climbed quickly out of the trunk and ran around to the other side of the car to hide.

The airline attendant was not being very understanding with Pops. "But I can't help you," he said. "We just don't have any more planes."

"Oh no?" said Pops. "Then what's that thing sitting out there, huh?"

He pointed out of the window at the runway. Sure enough, a propeller plane was parked there. Its motor was running, as if it was set to take off any minute.

"Don't tell me that's a bird!" Pops cried.

"No, sir, but that's a privately owned plane. I can't sell you a ticket for it. It's owned by Cruncher Block. It's supposed to be taking off any minute."

"Is that so?" Pops said.

At exactly that moment, a big man in a flashy white suit walked through the airline terminal, flanked on both sides by his bodyguards.

Pops watched the man head for the waiting plane.

Cruncher Block didn't even see Pops. His mind was still on the No-Limit World Race and the

Mammoth Car that was secretly carrying his gold. To his bodyguards, he said, "My special Motorcycle Mayhem Team failed to stop the Mach 5. But once we fly up there, I'll personally see that the job's done permanently. By me! Boys, the only person you can trust to see that a job's done right is yourself."

Spritle, still hiding on the airstrip, heard this loud and clear.

"Uh-oh," he whispered to Chim Chim. "We've got to stop that guy."

Cruncher Block took his sweet time climbing the steps of his plane. He was a big guy, and, if you asked him, there were a lot of steps.

Soon enough, he made it to his seat. He told the pilot to get the plane in the air. With that, the propellers started spinning. The plane took off into the night—and they were heading for Speed!

Cruncher Block smiled to himself in satisfaction. He had no idea that he and his men weren't alone on the plane. Hiding just behind the big seat where Cruncher Block had planted himself were

Spritle and Chim Chim.

Oblivious, Cruncher Block chuckled. "I always get hungry when I'm about to get more money," he bellowed. Then he turned to one of his assistants. "Get me a sandwich, would ya?"

His assistant brought out a good-size sandwich, but before Cruncher Block could get his meaty hands on it, two very small hands poked up from between the seats and grabbed the sandwich off the tray.

"You pig!" Cruncher Block bellowed at his assistant. "You ate my snack yourself!"

His assistant yelped, afraid to speak up.

The plane sped through the night, heading north to catch up to the race.

Even though it was nighttime, there was no time to stop driving. Speed wasn't stopping, and neither was the Mammoth Car.

The Mammoth Car drove up the mountain roads in the darkness, still in the lead. It came to a steep series of hills with many twists and turns and slowed down a little.

Trixie couldn't help but notice. "Look, Speed!" she cried. "The Mammoth Car looks like it's slowing down!"

"It must be too big and heavy for these mountain roads," Speed said. "Maybe now we'll get a chance to catch up to it."

Seeing his shot, Speed stepped down hard on the gas pedal.

The Mach 5 sped up the mountain roads, taking the steep climb and the swift curves with ease. Sure enough, they reached the tail of the Mammoth Car in no time. Speed maneuvered the Mach 5 around the Mammoth Car, gaining on it tire by mammoth tire. Within seconds, he had reached the first compartment of the Mammoth Car, the section that housed the Mammoth Car's driver.

The driver spotted the Mach 5 from his window. He hadn't even noticed the Mach 5 gaining on him until it was too late. He had to do something to get the Mach 5 out of this race, or Cruncher Block would be furious!

The Mammoth Car's driver turned the wheel and rammed the enormous weight of the Mammoth Car straight into the passenger side of the Mach 5. The impact sent the Mach 5 skidding off toward the side of the road. The Mach 5 bounced against the guardrail and boomeranged back at the Mammoth Car. It hit one of the Mammoth Car's giant tires, bouncing back at the guardrail again.

The Mach 5 was out of control!

Speed thought quickly. He pressed a button on the steering column, shooting the Mach 5 off the ground entirely to avoid a crash. The Mach 5 landed on a bed of rocks off the side of the road. Now he was out of harm's way, and the Mammoth Car couldn't knock him off the mountain. Speed activated the belt tires, and this time they took hold right away. He steered through the rocks, never slowing.

But the Mammoth Car was not about to give up on getting Speed out of this race.

The driver of the Mammoth Car took a swift

turn, barreling straight through the guardrail and leaping off the cliff and onto the rocks. He'd taken the Mammoth Car off the road to follow the Mach 5.

The Mammoth Car crashed through the rocky terrain, heading down the steep mountain with its bright headlights glaring.

"They're after us!" Trixie cried.

Speed took a look behind them. With the lights on in the night, the front of the Mammoth Car looked like the face of a monster. Speed kept going.

He turned onto a road, but the Mammoth Car followed.

Speed looked ahead toward a dark patch of woods. He pressed a button on the steering column, and rotary saws shot out of the front end of the Mach 5, ready to clear a straight path through the forest.

Speed didn't hesitate. He turned off the road into the dark mass of trees. The rotary saws cut

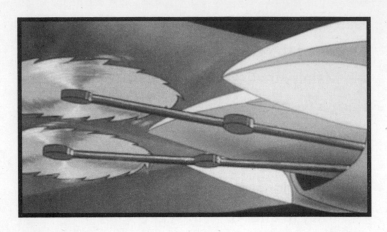

down any obstacles in his way. He kept driving.

"I think we'll be safe now," Trixie said. "The path we made will be too narrow for them to follow."

Then Trixie caught sight of the bright lights belonging to the Mammoth Car. It had its own saws, and it was cutting an enormous path for itself through the woods. Trees fell left and right, as if the entire forest was collapsing.

Speed took a quick look in the rearview mirror. "Here comes the Mammoth Car again!" he yelled. "I've got to find some way to stop it."

Speed thought for a moment. Then he spun

the Mach 5 around and headed right for the Mammoth Car.

"I'm going to try to rip up those tires," Speed told Trixie. Speed drove the Mach 5 right up to the gigantic tires and aimed the Mach 5's rotary saws at it. There was a sharp rip as the saws tore through a rubber tire. The tire flew off the axle and into the trees.

But the Mammoth Car had dozens of other tires, and still it kept going.

Speed did a swift U-turn and came at the Mammoth Car again, the rotary saws out. He cut open another tire, but the Mammoth Car butted him and knocked him in the other direction.

Then the Mammoth Car activated its plow and hurled a mountain of dirt at the Mach 5. Seeing it coming, Speed pressed a button on the steering column, and the Mach 5 jumped up several feet in the air. The mountain of dirt covered the ground where he'd been, but it didn't touch the Mach 5.

Speed had escaped being buried in the

mountain of dirt, but he still hadn't escaped the Mammoth Car. It was heading straight for him again, and the high jump had knocked the Mach 5 off balance, stalling it out.

The Mammoth Car started circling around the Mach 5. It circled and circled, so long and with so many segments that soon the Mach 5 was stuck in the center of a whirling red blur.

There was no way out.

The Mammoth Car kept driving in circles. The Mach 5 was trapped with nowhere to go.

"I'll try to get us out of this," Speed said. He hit a button that caused the Mach 5 to leap up and over the Mammoth Car. But the leap was too high and too wide, and before they knew it the Mach 5 had landed with a great splash in a nearby lake.

"Aaaah!" Speed and Trixie cried as the Mach 5 sunk into the lake. The Mach 5 was a car that could do many things . . . but could it pull Speed and Trixie from the depths of this lake? And, if so, would they be able to escape the Mammoth Car?

The driver of the Mammoth Car stood next to Lake Icy-Chill and looked out across it with great satisfaction. He'd seen the Mach 5 dive into the lake. He'd seen it plunge down to the bottom. And now many minutes had passed, and he had not seen it come back out.

The air bubbles had cleared. It looked as though there was no way the Mach 5 was getting out of its watery grave.

"That does it," the driver said to his crew. "Let's go."

They all climbed back into the Mammoth Car. One of the crew members called Cruncher Block on the radio. "We just sent the Mach 5 down to the bottom of Lake Icy-Chill," he reported to their boss.

With that, they drove out of the forest and

back toward the road that would lead them to the finish line of the No-Limit World Race.

But maybe they had spoken too soon.

Because as soon as the Mammoth Car was out of sight, a narrow rod shot up from the center of the lake. It swiveled around, casting its eye on the surrounding area.

Down at the bottom of the lake, safe inside the Mach 5's closed cockpit, Speed and Trixie were waiting and watching. The long rod was the Mach 5's periscope, and they were using it to make sure the coast was clear.

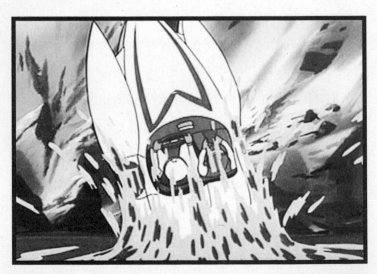

"The Mammoth Car is gone," Speed said. "Now it'll be safe to get out of here. Let's go!"

He pressed a button on the steering column to close the periscope.

Then he gunned the engine and sped the Mach 5 through the lake's sandy bottom. With all the technological advances designed in the Mach 5, of course there would be no problem with it driving through water!

The Mach 5 burst out of the lake and sped through the forest back toward the road. As Speed drove, Trixie took out a small voice recorder and made this message:

"This is Trixie in the Mach 5, calling Inspector Detector. Speed and I have found out that the Mammoth Car is not just a racer. They tried to sink us at the bottom of a lake! They're trying to stop us from finding out some very important secrets about the car. We'll stay in the race for as long as we can, but please investigate the Mammoth Car as soon as possible!"

Speed cut in to add, "We think it may be carrying the fifty million dollars in gold bars stolen from the National Bank!"

"I can't think of anything else to add, can you?" Trixie asked Speed.

"We've told him all we know," Speed said.

Satisfied with the message, Trixie inserted the miniature audio tape into the homing robot. It was banged up from its previous run-in with the Mammoth Car, but it was still usable. Speed hit the button that sent the homing robot, message safely inside, out into the sky. The coordinates that were set would lead the homing robot straight to Inspector Detector, who would be waiting at the checkpoint.

Trixie looked up into the night sky. "That message is important," she said. "I sure hope it makes it."

High overhead, Cruncher Block's plane soared through the deep night. He had his pilot follow the road that was being used for the No-Limit World Race, to try to catch up to the Mammoth Car so he could keep an eye on it.

"Hey, look at that, boss," his assistant said.

"Shut up," Cruncher Block yelled. "I know the scenery's gorgeous. I don't want to hear about it."

"But I'm not looking at the scenery, boss, I'm looking at the Mach 5."

Cruncher Block forced his way over to the window. "You're dreaming," he said. But then he saw it with his own two eyes. Sure enough, the Mach 5 was on the road below.

"That's no dream," his assistant said. "That's a nightmare."

"I thought they sunk that little car at the

bottom of a lake," Cruncher Block said.

"They did, but that's the Mach 5, all right," his assistant said.

"I don't believe it," Cruncher Block yelled. "Fly closer!"

His pilot heeded the command and dove the plane toward the Mach 5.

Speed and Trixie saw something come straight at them from the sky. They swerved and ducked on reflex.

"That pilot should learn to fly better," Speed said.

"I think they did it on purpose," Trixie said.

Up in the plane, Cruncher Block stomped toward the cockpit. "I wanna talk to the Mammoth Car," he told the copilot. He grabbed the radio.

"Now listen, you stoneheads," he yelled into the radio. "I told you to get rid of those two nosy kids. Can't you do a simple job like that? What went wrong, huh?"

"Nothin' went wrong," one of the members

of the Mammoth Car said from down below. "We knocked those kids into the lake, just like we told you."

"Oh yeah?" Cruncher Block yelled into the radio.

The crewman on the other end flinched.

"Look behind ya!" Cruncher raged. "And don't you tell me that's a ghost!"

The crewman looked out the window to get a good look.

That's when he saw it: the sleek white race car following behind the Mammoth Car, just as before. Just like it had never sunk to the bottom of the lake!

"Aaaah!" the crewman yelped. "It's the Mach 5! But how'd they get out of that lake?"

Cruncher Block didn't have time to speculate. And he didn't care. What mattered was getting his Mammoth Car—and his gold—across the finish line and out of the country.

"Now listen carefully," he told his crewman over the radio. "The Mammoth Car will be stopping at our secret fueling point any minute. Our men are waiting for you, and they'll refuel the car. But they'll also take care of the Mach 5. So make sure that it follows you there."

The driver couldn't help but butt in on the conversation. "But they could learn our secret!" he cried to Cruncher Block.

"Do as I say," Cruncher Block yelled back.

Then Cruncher's plane rose up out of sight as it flew away.

Taking orders, the Mammoth Car's driver

turned off the road, hoping the Mach 5 would follow.

Inside the Mach 5, Trixie turned to Speed. "I wonder where the Mammoth Car is headed," she said.

"If we follow them, maybe we can find out what they're up to," Speed said. He took the same turn, following the Mammoth Car off the road.

Unknown to Speed—and unknown to Cruncher Block and the Mammoth Car—Racer X took the same turn and followed them all.

Speed drove the Mach 5 along a dirt road lined with boulders following the Mammoth Car. But the Mammoth Car had a head start, and Speed had lost sight of it. A mountainous wall of rock climbed high into the sky, hiding the early morning sun. At the end of the long dirt road was an abandoned mine. Old, broken-down machinery littered the area. A dark entrance to the mine gaped open in front of Speed. Nobody was around for miles. And the Mammoth Car was nowhere to be seen.

"Hmm," Speed said to Trixie. "I don't see anybody here. This place seems deserted."

"Uh-huh," Trixie said. She looked out the window, looking for some sign of the Mammoth Car.

Suddenly, she spotted something. "A plane!" she cried.

Sure enough, a small charter plane was parked beside the entrance to the mine. It seemed to be empty. Little did Trixie know that this was the same plane that had just been carrying Cruncher Block and his men.

Speed pulled the Mach 5 closer to the small plane. "That's funny," he said. "Let's take a look."

Speed and Trixie got out of the car and took a few steps toward the plane. That's when they noticed the shadows in the dirt. They weren't alone after all! A group of men stood nearby; their long shadows looked gigantic in the sunlight. They started advancing on Speed and Trixie.

"Run!" Speed cried. He grabbed Trixie's hand and they took off. The closest place to hide was the entrance to the abandoned mine shaft. They rushed inside.

But the men didn't follow them into the mine.

One of the men raised his hand to stop the

others from going in. "No need to go in! They're trapped in there!" he yelled to the others. He gave the man near the mining cart tracks a thumbs-up. "Let 'er roll!" he commanded.

At that signal, the man released the brake on the mining cart. It was heavy, full of coal and steel poles that stuck out every which way. With great speed, it began to roll down the track...straight into the mine shaft where Speed and Trixie were hiding!

Inside the mine, the mining cart raced down the track, its long steel poles grinding into the walls of the mine shaft and causing some of the supports in the walls to break.

Speed and Trixie cried out in alarm and jumped up out of the way before it could run them over. But when they came down, they landed on top of the mining cart itself, which was racing deeper and deeper down the tracks and into the lower reaches of the mine. There was no way to stop the cart, and there was nowhere else to jump. The narrow mine shaft led down through the dark tunnels until all of a sudden . . .

There was a bright light! The mining cart had reached the end of the tracks, revealing a hidden cave where the Mammoth Car was parked. It must have driven in through another entrance. The

bright lights were the Mammoth Car's enormous headlights.

There was no way to keep the mining cart from stopping violently. It flung Speed and Trixie off into the dirt of the cave in front of the Mammoth Car. They were knocked unconscious.

Meanwhile, Spritle and his pet chimpanzee, Chim Chim, were still stowed away on the small plane parked outside the mine shaft. With all of Cruncher Block's men busy with Speed and Trixie, Spritle saw their chance to get off the plane and help.

"Don't make a sound, Chim Chim," he warned his pal. "We don't want anyone to know we're here."

They hid for a moment under the plane and then raced for cover behind some abandoned mining equipment.

Chim Chim pointed toward the mine shaft and grunted in alarm.

"Shhh!" Spritle warned him. "Those men are going to do something bad to Speed and Trixie!"

Chim Chim shivered.

Spritle and Chim Chim watched the men guarding the Mach 5.

"I've got to help my brother!" Spritle said.

Chim Chim quietly hooted his agreement. He had had enough! He could not let those men hurt Speed or Trixie, or even the Mach 5! Suddenly, he leaped out of the shadows and flung himself, hooting and screeching, at one of the bad men. But the man turned around quickly and knocked Chim Chim to the ground. He was much, much bigger than Chim Chim had expected.

"Aaaah!" cried Spritle.

Spritle and Chim Chim ran screaming into the mine shaft. Then they fell, head over heels, down the steep slope until they landed on the tracks. None of the men raced into the mine shaft after them.

Spritle and Chim Chim tried to keep quiet as they crawled toward the light. There, around the corner, they could see Speed and Trixie. They had been tied to a mining cart. And they were surrounded by the crew of the Mammoth Car!

Speed and Trixie woke to find themselves tied to a mining cart in a large cavern with the Mammoth Car.

It was some kind of secret hideout. The Mammoth Car was hooked up to a large gas tank.

Trixie glared at the men holding them captive. "What do you plan to do with us?" she yelled to them.

An enormous man wearing a bright white suit and hat walked into the cavern. He was Cruncher Block.

"I'll tell ya," he boomed in Trixie's direction. "So you've found my secret place, eh? Well, I'm finished with this secret headquarters, so I'm gonna get rid of it, and the two of you while I'm at it!"

Speed stared him down. But there was little

he could do, tied up with rope as he was.

"Yeah, that's what I'm gonna do," Cruncher Block yelled. "And it'll be way more interesting than just knocking ya into Lake Icy-Chill!"

"Why, I'll . . ." Speed mumbled. He was shaking with anger.

"What do you think is in that cart you're tied to?" Cruncher Block bellowed. "Three tons of dynamite!"

Trixie gasped in horror.

"Yeah, that's right," Cruncher Block continued. "Once we light that fuse, we're going to push that cart down into the deepest levels of the mine." He laughed heartily. "Somewhere deep down in that tunnel the fuse is gonna set off the dynamite, and that'll be the end of both of you. Then nobody will learn what you found out about my Mammoth Car. Too bad you have to lose the race, and your lives." He laughed some more. His loud laughter echoed sinisterly throughout the mine shaft.

Then he tipped his shiny white hat and said good-bye.

⚫ ⚫ ⚫ ⚫

Outside the mine, Cruncher Block's men had orders to destroy the Mach 5 and get rid of all the evidence that Speed and Trixie had ever been here. But first they wanted to have some fun with the race car.

A man held an ax up to the clean white exterior of the car.

"Ready!" one of the men called.

"Cut it!" cried another.

The man was just about to lower the ax when a hand reached out from nowhere and grabbed it away from him. "No you don't!" a voice said. The man that had been holding the ax was flipped over and knocked hard to the ground.

Then all the other men were knocked out, too.

Racer X had come again at just the right moment. He'd saved the Mach 5, but could he save Speed and Trixie?

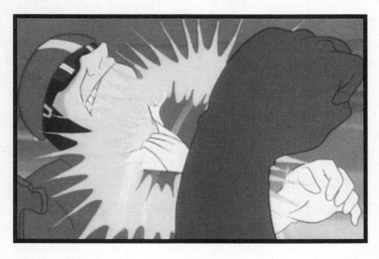

Back in the mine shaft, Cruncher Block left his men so they could light the dynamite fuse and get rid of Speed and Trixie. But before they did, they made sure to have the Mammoth Car driven out of the mine shaft. It had to get back to the No-Limit World Race. With the Mach 5 out of the picture, the Mammoth Car would win the race for sure. And by staying in the race until the finish line, it would make it over the border and out of the country.

Down in the mine, Speed and Trixie were still tied to the mining cart.

"Now!" one of Cruncher Block's men ordered. "Light the fuse!"

Speed and Trixie were in total shock.

A man lit the fuse and undid the brake on the cart. Then the men ran out of the mine, leaving

Speed and Trixie to fend for themselves.

With the brake no longer keeping the cart in place, it began to inch forward along the tracks. The fuse hissed. The cart picked up speed, carrying them deeper and deeper into the mine. There was no stopping it now.

But as they turned the corner, something—or someone—landed on top of the mining cart. It was Spritle and Chim Chim. They'd been hiding around the bend and had been waiting for their chance to help Speed and Trixie.

"It's you!" Speed cried, startled.

Spritle and Chim Chim knocked the dynamite off of the cart.

Then Chim Chim gnawed at the ropes that were holding Speed. With his sharp teeth, he was able to set Speed free in no time. But when the rope broke, Spritle, who was trying to untie Trixie on the other side, lost control. Spritle started swinging in wild circles all around the mining cart as it gained even more speed.

"Yow!" Spritle cried. He was accidentally winding the rope back around Speed and Trixie!

The rope was holding, and the cart was quickly rolling toward a head-on collision with another cart. It seemed like there was nothing anyone could do to stop it.

Just then Racer X came running in! Racer X hit a switch on the tracks, diverting the runaway cart that Speed and Trixie were tied to so that they sped down another line of tracks and missed hitting the other cart. Then Racer X quickly leaped onto the cart with Speed, Trixie, Spritle, and Chim Chim.

"Huh?!" Speed said.

Racer X expertly undid the ropes, setting everyone free. "You just avoided that crash," Racer X said.

"I don't know how you got down here, Racer X," Speed said. "Or how you even knew to find

us, but thank you for switching those rails in the nick of time."

"You saved us," Trixie gushed.

"We're not out of the mine yet," Racer X said. He turned the cart on the tracks and started heading for the exit.

As they approached the mouth of the mine, the dynamite that had been knocked off the mining cart earlier exploded in the distance with a loud burst of noise and falling rocks.

"And you two saved us also," Trixie said to Spritle and Chim Chim. "If you hadn't knocked the dynamite off of the cart, I don't want to think what could have happened."

"We were very lucky today," Speed said.

They emerged from the mine, all in one piece.

"If I hadn't arrived, you would never have gotten out of that mine," Racer X said. "Cruncher Block and his men will do anything to win."

"Chim Chim and I were hiding on that plane,"

Spritle said. "That's how we found Speed. But I don't get it, Racer X, how did you know where to find us?"

Racer X didn't answer.

"You always seem to arrive when we need you the most," Trixie added.

Speed was staring intently at Racer X. There was something about him that was so . . . familiar. Racer X was a famous race car driver. He always wore a mask. But even so, even with the mask on, there was something odd about Racer X that Speed couldn't put his finger on.

He sort of reminds me of my big brother, Rex, Speed thought.

Racer X turned and saw Speed staring at him. "Is something the matter, Speed?" he asked. "You're looking at me strangely. What's going on?"

No, Speed thought. *That would be impossible. There's no way my brother Rex and Racer X are the same person.*

Little did Speed know that his hunch was right.

"Nothing's the matter," Speed said. "I'm just thinking of the race."

"And look," Spritle said. "The Mach 5 is fine. Those bad men didn't hurt your car at all, Speed!"

The Mach 5 was unharmed and parked just where Speed had left it. There wasn't a scratch on it—thanks to Racer X.

Racer X was now the one staring intently at Speed. "I hope you never leave your car in the middle of a race again," he said. "Now hurry! You may be able to catch up to the Mammoth Car."

Speed nodded. Racer X was right; he never should have left the Mach 5. "Thanks for everything, Racer X," he said. Then he shook thoughts of his brother Rex out of his mind and hopped in his car with Trixie.

THE RACE GOES ON

Cruncher Block was flying through the clouds in his plane. He gazed out the window at the ground far below and grinned.

"Now we should have no more trouble," he said.

Then a radio signal cut in.

"This is the Mammoth Car calling Cruncher Block," came a voice over the radio. "Did you get rid of those kids? We're running right on schedule."

Cruncher Block went to the window again. Through the clouds, down on the road beneath the plane, he could see the long Mammoth Car speeding along the highway. It was a red blur, steadily moving toward the finish line as planned.

"Yes. They won't be bothering us ever again," Cruncher Block boomed into the radio. "You finish

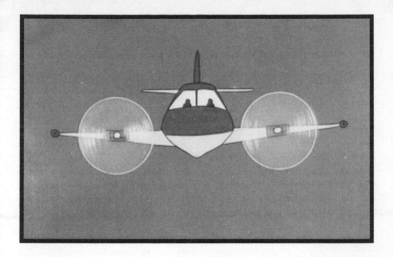

that race, and then we'll meet you at the boat."

The plane picked up speed and swooped away from the road, heading for the pier where Cruncher Block's boat was waiting.

Meanwhile, Speed and Trixie were making good time on the road. They were back in the No-Limit World Race, keeping their eyes peeled for the Mammoth Car in the distance. They hoped they could still catch up.

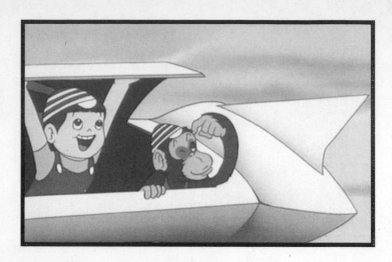

They raced all day and all through the night in the Mach 5, and they passed the ocean just as the sun was rising over the water.

Sprinkle and Chim Chim were riding comfortably in the Mach 5's trunk. They opened the trunk to peek out at the sky as the sun came up. "Morning!" Sprinkle said to Chim Chim. "It looks like it's going to be a great day."

Chim Chim gazed at the sun and hooted his agreement.

The Mach 5 raced over sandy beaches and down seaside roads. It could win this race yet.

At the checkpoint, Pops Racer and Inspector Detector were waiting anxiously for the Mach 5 to arrive. A group of racing officials stood by, ready to give each of the cars still in the No-Limit World Race an official stamp to keep going. A crowd of onlookers sat in the stands, watching the road. No cars had reached the checkpoint yet.

Then a motor could be heard in the distance. Pops craned his neck to see who was approaching. The motor got louder and louder—it could only belong to the biggest of all the cars in the race.

The Mammoth Car came into view, its tires taller than most cars. The crowd oohed and aahed at its amazing red bulk and its many segments. They waved up at the driver as the huge car slowed to a stop at the checkpoint. Dark black smoke billowed out from its front grille as the engine quieted.

Over the loudspeaker, the announcer told the crowd, "This is the first car to reach the checkpoint!" The crowd cheered wildly.

Using a very tall ladder, a racing official climbed up to the window. "So far the Mammoth Car's winning!" he announced to the driver.

"Well, of course we are," the driver snapped. "And we're gonna win the whole race. Now stamp the certificate with the time that we reached here. And don't you lie."

The racing official stamped the Mammoth Car's certificate with the correct time. "Now why would I lie?" he said. "You're in the lead!" Then he climbed down the ladder to the ground far below.

The Mammoth Car started its mammoth engine. A rumbling growl filled the area. Black smoke exploded again from the front grille.

Then someone walked in front of the Mammoth Car to keep it from going anywhere. It was Inspector Detector. He held up his hand before the towering hood. "Hold it!" he yelled.

Inside the Mammoth Car, the driver and his assistant driver exchanged glances.

"The police!" the assistant driver mumbled. "What do you think they want?"

Inspector Detector answered for him. "We want to inspect the car," he called. "We think you might be smuggling." Two other police officers stood beside him.

"Again?!" snapped the driver. He rolled his eyes. Then he called down to Inspector Detector. "Go ahead, mate. We got nothin' to hide."

"Yeah!" called the assistant driver. "You looked already, but look again if you wanna."

The driver pushed a button on the dashboard, and a door in the first compartment opened. A stairway slid down so the officers could climb inside.

Inspector Detector turned to the two officers with him. "Inspect everything carefully," he told them. "Don't miss a single thing. Now go ahead. Get in there!"

At the wheel, the driver and his assistant driver waited impatiently. The police officers were taking their time getting their equipment together. This inspection would take forever. Then the driver saw a flash of white in his side-view mirror.

"No!" he cried. "It's Speed Racer!"

The Mach 5, with Speed at the wheel, was swiftly approaching the checkpoint.

"What?!" the assistant driver cried. "I thought the boss took care of him!"

The crowd cheered even louder as the Mach 5 pulled up to a stop beside the Mammoth Car.

Inspector Detector hurried over to it. "Speed

Racer, I'm so glad to see you!"

Speed stood straight up in his seat and pointed at the Mammoth Car. "Inspector, you'd better make a thorough inspection of the Mammoth Car!"

Pops ran up, waving the Mach 5's homing robot. The homing robot had reached its destination, just as Speed and Trixie had hoped!

"He's already doing it!" Pops said to Speed. "Thanks to you. We got your message!"

"Pops!" Speed said, surprised. "I didn't know you'd be here. And we've got Spritle and Chim Chim with us in the Mach 5."

Now it was Pops's turn to be surprised. "Huh?!" he said. He headed for the Mach 5's trunk, but just before he reached it Spritle and Chim Chim jumped out and ran away. Pops found an empty trunk. "Speed, I don't see them. Where are the little rascals?"

"They're both in the trunk," Speed called.

"No they're not," Pops said. "There isn't anybody back here, Speed."

But before Speed could get out to look for himself, he heard a man yell beside him, "Clear the road!"

"The big car's leaving!" Speed said.

Sure enough, the engine roared and a burst of dark smoke rose out over the roadway. The Mammoth Car's driver had decided to leave before the inspection was over. The stairway pulled up, knocking the police officers who were just climbing out of the back off onto the ground below. The door to the Mammoth Car's interior closed. And with that, the Mammoth Car sped away.

As it did, two small figures could be seen hanging onto the back end of the giant Mammoth Car.

"That's Spritle and Chim Chim!" Speed cried.

Pops started running. "Stop that car!" he yelled.

Inspector Detector and the police officers started running, too. "Stop!" he yelled to the Mammoth Car. "Stop!"

But the Mammoth Car did not stop. Instead, it sped up and was soon out on the road where no one could chase it.

Except for the Mach 5.

"Hang on, Trixie," Speed said. "We're going after it!"

A racing official ran up to Trixie's window and quickly stamped the official racing paperwork. "Not before we're sure you're still in the race!" he yelled.

"Hurry, Speed!" Trixie yelled.

The Mach 5 took off in pursuit of the Mammoth Car.

Inside the Mammoth Car, Spritle and Chim Chim looked around the empty chamber.

"That's funny," Spritle said. "Don't you think so, Chim Chim?"

Chim Chim grunted. He did think it was quite funny.

"What's that?" Spritle said, noticing a button in the wall. He pushed it, and a door slid open to reveal one of the Mammoth Car's driving crew—a big thug of a man—towering over them.

Spritle gasped.

The thug laughed sinisterly.

Meanwhile, Speed and Trixie were speeding along the road trying to catch up to the Mammoth

Car. Speed had the giant red car in his sights. "We'll be able to catch them soon, Trixie," he said.

"Oh, good," she said.

In the Mammoth Car, the driver and his assistant were speeding along, unaware that they had two small stowaways onboard.

"In a few minutes, we'll be at the boat," the driver told his assistant.

But a police helicopter was also speeding overhead. It was quickly gaining on the Mammoth Car below. Inspector Detector and Pops looked out

the window. The Mammoth Car and the Mach 5 were side by side on the road.

"They're getting close to the finish line," Inspector Detector told Pops.

"Good," Pops said. "Then they won't be able to go any farther. They'll reach the finish line and you'll arrest them."

⊚   ⊚   ⊚   ⊚

The crowd at the finish line of the No-Limit World Race was much larger than the crowd had been at the checkpoint, or even at the start of the race. There were thousands of people in the stands, all waiting to see who would cross the finish first and be the lucky car to win the longest race in the world. An announcer sat high up in a black-and-white checkered lookout. Over the loudspeaker he kept the crowd informed. "As they come into the home stretch, the Mammoth Car and the Mach 5 are tied for first place!" he cried.

The crowd hushed as the two contenders approached the finish line.

The announcer continued, "Only a few seconds, and the great No-Limit World Race will be all over!"

The Mammoth Car and the Mach 5 sped forward.

"Here they come!" yelled the announcer. The crowd buzzed with excitement.

The Mammoth Car and the Mach 5 both burst forward toward the finish line, where a man stood waving a black-and-white-checkered flag.

"They're at the finish line!" the announcer yelled. "And as they cross it, they're in a dead

heat. It's an absolute tie for first place!"

The Mach 5 and the Mammoth Car were tied, nose to nose. There was no clear way to call a winner.

The crowd roared. The applause was deafening.

The announcer continued, "It may be the momentum from the speed at which both cars have been racing, but they haven't slowed down! The Mammoth Car is going even faster than before!"

Sure enough, though it had crossed the finish line, the Mammoth Car showed no sign of stopping. It had sped up and was shooting ahead as if the race was still on.

Confused but determined, Speed kept driving, too.

The Mammoth Car and the Mach 5 left the roars of the crowd behind. They were still racing, but it wasn't to win any race. Something else was going on.

Inside the cavernous segments of the Mammoth Car, Spritle and Chim Chim were tied up with rope and hanging from the ceiling so that they couldn't cause any trouble or try to escape.

Spritle tried to negotiate with the thug who had tied them up. "We won't do anything. Cut the rope. Please let us go."

The thug looked up at them and sighed. "You'll behave yourselves?" he asked.

"We will! We will!" Spritle said. "I promise we won't do anything we shouldn't."

"Okay, then," the thug said. He lowered the rope so Spritle and Chim Chim were on the ground. But before he could cut the rope and set them free, Spritle and Chim Chim ran a swift circle around him, catching his ankle in the rope and tripping him. The thug fell with a loud thump, flat on his face.

"We had to do that," Spritle told Chim Chim. "So, see? I kept my word."

⊙　⊙　⊙　⊙

Not minutes later, a funny-looking thug in the Mammoth Car's red crew uniform walked through the long length of the Mammoth Car toward the front, where the driver sat.

He was walking strangely.

His legs didn't seem to connect properly to his body. His arms flopped around in empty sleeves.

He wobbled. His helmet was way too big. And his face looked like a monkey's.

It was Spritle and Chim Chim in disguise!

Chim Chim had climbed on top of Spritle's shoulders, and they had stolen the thug's uniform to make it seem like they were a big, tall man. Now they just had to keep anyone from looking at them too closely.

When one of the Mammoth Car's real crew members happened to pass Spritle and Chim Chim, he waved and smiled as usual and then did a double take. Had he just said hello to a monkey?

Before he could figure it out, Chim Chim conked him on the head with a wrench.

They kept moving through the Mammoth Car's compartments. Whenever a Mammoth Car crew member would emerge, Chim Chim and Spritle found a way to stop him. Once they reached the head of the Mammoth Car, they'd figure out a way to get control of the huge vehicle and help Spritle's big brother, Speed.

The Mammoth Car came into sight. It had reached the docks, where the ship Cruncher Block had sent was waiting. Cruncher Block himself had come to the docks to make sure that his precious Mammoth Car made it on the ship as planned.

But just beside the Mammoth Car was the Mach 5. Speed had caught up to them. Both the Mammoth Car and the Mach 5 came to a stop on the docks.

Cruncher Block growled when he saw the Mach 5. "Those two kids are still with `em," he said. He stood with his men on the deck of a giant ship that was tied to the dock.

"Don't worry, I'll cut them off," one of Cruncher Block's men called up from below. He hopped in his car and barreled over to the Mach 5, forcing Speed to go into reverse to avoid a collision. Cruncher Block's man wouldn't let up. He rammed the Mach 5 sideways to the edge of the dock. Speed almost skidded off into the ocean.

Meanwhile, the Mammoth Car was headed straight for the large ship. A giant door—large enough to fit a vehicle as big as the Mammoth Car—had opened in the cargo hold of the ship.

The Mammoth Car sped for it, but just seconds before it reached the giant doorway, it made a sharp right turn and sped away from the ship.

Cruncher Block looked down in alarm. "What happened?" he yelled. "Why didn't it come on the boat?"

Cruncher Block was thoroughly confused. The Mammoth Car was now driving away.

Inside the Mammoth Car, Spritle and Chim Chim had reached the driver's seat. They stood behind the driver menacingly, and Spritle spoke in a deep, low voice. Thinking a big giant man had come to take over, the driver was shaking in his boots and did whatever the man said. That's why he'd turned away from the ship—the scary man had told him to.

Chim Chim was still on Spritle's shoulders. "Good," Spritle said in the big, scary man's voice. "Now keep the Mammoth Car going straight. And no monkey business!"

That's when the driver looked into the rearview mirror and caught sight of the big, scary man's face for the first time. He looked just like a monkey!

"Wh-wh-who are you?" the driver stuttered.

The monkey-man had crazy red-rimmed eyes that scared him.

"Eeeeee-e-eeee-eeee!" the monkey-man responded.

"Monkey business!" the driver burst out. He turned in his seat to get a good look behind him. Chim Chim conked him on the head with the wrench.

The driver collapsed—which was good, because now Chim Chim and Spritle had full control of the Mammoth Car.

But that was also very, very bad . . . because neither one knew how to drive it!

"How do we stop the car?" Spritle cried. "We've got to find the brakes and use them."

Spritle and Chim Chim hopped behind the wheel, but the Mammoth Car was harder to steer than they thought. The brake was far down on the floor, and they couldn't reach it. The Mammoth Car veered wildly from left to right. Its long length whipped back and forth like a dizzy centipede. Spritle and Chim Chim clung to the steering wheel, trying to keep from flying out of the driver's seat.

"I've gotta reach the brake or we're gonna crash!" Spritle cried. "Hang on!" He tried stretching out his leg to find the brake, but his legs weren't long enough.

Outside, Cruncher Block and his men had left the ship and were running toward the retreating Mammoth Car.

"Stop!" Cruncher Block yelled. "Stop the car before it crashes!"

At the wheel, Spritle yelled. "Help! We're heading right for that big oil tank."

Chim Chim hooted in panic.

A gigantic oil tank was straight ahead—and the Mammoth Car was about to ram into it. If it did, the oil tank would blow up!

Back in the Mach 5, Speed and Trixie had gotten free from Cruncher Block's driver, and were staring at the out of control Mammoth Car in alarm.

"Something's wrong with the Mammoth Car!" Trixie cried. "It's going to crash into that oil tank!"

Sprtile and Chim Chim caught sight of the

Mach 5 in the Mammoth Car's side-view mirror. The Mach 5 was driving up alongside them. "Help us, Speed!" Spritle cried, hoping his big brother would save him.

Somehow, Speed knew to help.

He kept driving and turned to Trixie. "You've gotta take the wheel, Trixie," he said. She grabbed it, and Speed leaped over her to the passenger seat. Speed jumped up and grabbed hold of the Mammoth Car's ladder. Then he jumped up on it and started climbing toward the window.

When he jumped into the car, he found Spritle and Chim Chim driving. "Spritle!" he cried.

"Speed, we're going to crash!" Spritle cried.

Speed leaped into the driver's seat—the big oil tank straight ahead—and took control of the Mammoth Car. "Hang on!" he yelled as he stomped his foot on the brake.

Cruncher Block, who was watching from afar, yelled, "This is gonna be the end of my Mammoth Car!"

But Speed wasn't giving up yet. He slammed the brake again and hoped the Mammoth Car would stop in time. It skidded, its many tires squealing as it slowed just a few feet from the oil tank. It stopped, but not before hitting the side of the oil tank. Oil burst out and exploded—the Mammoth Car was engulfed in flames!

Trixie screamed. She stopped the Mach 5 and jumped out of the car.

The Mammoth Car's crew ran from the flaming wreck—they had gotten out safely. And soon, Speed was seen running out of the flames, Spritle and Chim Chim tucked in his arms. Trixie grabbed him. They stood off to the side, watching the fire surround the Mammoth Car.

Something strange was happening to the Mammoth Car. It seemed to be melting.

The entire body of the car was turning to gold liquid mush. After a few minutes, all that remained of the Mammoth Car was a gigantic pile of molten gold and some tires. The gold gleamed in the light from the flames.

"How can that be?" Trixie said.

"The Mammoth Car must have been made entirely of gold!" Speed said. "It wasn't smuggling gold bars out of the country at all—it *was* the gold bars!"

Fire trucks had arrived to fight the blaze. And the police had come as well, bringing Inspector Detector to arrest Cruncher Block.

Cruncher Block was howling to himself. "My plan is ruined," he cried. "I could have gotten that stolen gold out of the country, but not now. Not

now!" He started for the wreckage, but Inspector Detector held him back.

"Don't go any closer," he said. "There could be more explosions."

"My car," Cruncher Block mumbled to himself. "My golden car."

Another explosion lit up the sky, destroying what remained of the Mammoth Car.

A SWEET REWARD

Later, at the finish line for the No-Limit World Race, photographers surrounded the Go Team, snapping pictures of Speed holding the trophy high in the air. Trixie stood at his side, beaming. Speed laughed and smiled from the winner's box. Not only did the Mammoth Car not win, but its smuggling secret was uncovered and the greedy Cruncher Block was behind bars where he belonged.

Inspector Detector pushed through the throng of photographers. "Congratulations, Speed," he said, shaking Speed's hand. "You certainly drove a great race."

"Yeah, congratulations, Speed," Sparky said, joining them. "And you, too, Trixie. You were the best assistant driver for this race."

"Thanks, Sparky," Trixie said.

Pops Racer walked over and stood beside

Inspector Detector, gazing proudly at his son. "The Mammoth Car was disqualified," he said. "So even though the race was a tie, the Mach 5 has been declared the winner!" He turned to Speed and Trixie. "You both did a great job," he told them. His smile was enormous.

"And besides," Inspector Detector added, "you found the stolen gold!"

"Ahem!" came a loud voice from down below. Inspector Detector looked down toward his feet to find Spritle and Chim Chim standing there with stony looks on their faces.

"Well, what's the matter?" Inspector Detector asked Spritle. "Why do you look so upset?"

Spritle spoke with his arms crossed over his chest. "Some people get rewards, and some people get nothing at all. Even though they deserve a medal, at least." Spritle and Chim Chim climbed up on the winner's box, taking the second-place spot as though it was theirs all along.

Pops leaned in to Inspector Detector. "They're just jealous," he whispered into the detective's ear. "But maybe if you give them some little thing, they won't be so hurt."

"Hmm," Inspector Detector said to himself. Then, raising his voice, he said to Spritle and Chim Chim, "And both of you have also done a very fine job." He found a smaller, but shiny, gold trophy and brought it over to them. "Here. Please accept this small token of our gratitude."

Even though the trophy was just as shiny and almost as nice as Speed's, Spritle shrugged, unimpressed. Chim Chim wrinkled his nose.

"Is that all we get?" Spritle said. "Just a shiny gold trophy?"

Inspector Detector acted surprised.

"We were hoping for some candy," Spritle explained.

Pops chuckled heartily.

Inspector Detector broke out into a smile. "Well then," he said. "Why don't you reach inside?"

"Huh?" said Spritle. Chim Chim sniffed the air and his eyes lit up. They shoved their hands inside the shiny gold trophy and pulled out fistsfuls of candy!

"Ahhhhhh!" was all Spritle could say. He and Chim Chim shoved the candy in their mouths and danced around with glee. They ate so much, they saw stars!

And Speed, Trixie, Sparky, Pops, and Inspector Detector watched the feast, laughing. Now what could be a bigger reward than that?

The No-Limit World Race wasn't the only time I was in an offtrack race. And that sure was awfully tricky of the Mammoth Car's team to hide the stolen gold in the shape of a car, wasn't it? Who would've thought they'd go to all that trouble? Sometimes thieves will hide things in the strangest places!

This reminds me of the time I raced in the Pineapple Grand Prix . . . You won't believe it when I tell you what was found, and where.

Read on!

Part One:
The Pineapple Strategy

Speed Racer was in South America ready to compete in the Pineapple Grand Prix, the most prestigious car race in the Southern Hemisphere. The prize was an enormous amount of money, but Speed wasn't in it for that. He wanted to master the mysterious, unfamiliar course that was like no race he'd ever driven in before.

The night before the race, Speed, Sparky, Trixie, Spritle, and Chim Chim met in their hotel to go over strategy.

Speed spread a large map across the table so the team could get a sense of the course.

"According to this map, part of the course runs through some of the most dangerous and unexplored territory in the Southern Hemisphere," Speed said, pointing to the area on the map. "And it ends after we go through this area called the Valley of Destruction."

"I'm not sure I like that name. It's frightening," Trixie said.

"So is the racecourse, I bet. It'll be tough," added Sparky.

"I'm afraid you're right. Not many will finish. At least that's what I heard," Trixie said as she leaned in for a closer look at the map. "And to make things more difficult, there's the matter of the pineapples."

"What's that?" Spritle called. "Does the winner get pineapples when he crosses the finish line? Chim Chim and I love pineapples."

"Well, sure, I think you do win some pineapples, Spritle," Speed said, chuckling. "But since the pineapple is the national fruit of this country, each driver will carry a pineapple with him during the race. The winner will be the first car to cross the finish line. But if a driver has lost his pineapple, he'll be disqualified!"

"Speed, you'll be the first to cross the finish line," Spritle said confidently. "And then when you do, Chim Chim and I will eat your pineapple!"

"Sure thing, Spritle," Speed said.

Suddenly there was a knock at the hotel room door. When Trixie opened it, a local girl who was probably about sixteen years old stood on the other side. She had pale hair and seemed very frail.

"Excuse me," she said in a soft voice. She spoke in English, but in the accent of her country. "I am looking for Mr. Speed Racer."

Speed stepped up to the door. "Hello," he said. "I'm Speed Racer. Please come in."

The girl entered the room and lowered her eyes sadly. "My name is Eloisa Hazard," she said softly. "I am the sister of Hap Hazard, one of the drivers who will be competing against you tomorrow."

Speed gave Trixie a look. He wasn't sure what this visit was all about.

"More than anything in the world, I want to see my brother win the Grand Prix, so won't you let him win?" Eloisa asked quickly. She raised her eyes to Speed and held them for a long moment, pleading with him.

"You're asking me to lose the Grand Prix?" Speed said, astonished.

"Yes. My brother wants you to lose and so do I, Speed," Eloisa said. "We have heard how good a race car driver you are, and we know you came all this way to win this race. But can't you win another race in your own country? Can't you let my brother win this race, please?"

"But that would be cheating!" Speed exclaimed. "I never cheat!"

"But it would mean so much to my brother and me. If he wins he'll have the chance to become the manager of a big factory that builds cars. Winning that race is all that matters to my poor brother," Eloisa pleaded. "Please lose the race tomorrow, Speed."

"I must ask you to leave," Speed said in a cold voice. He was insulted. He always raced fair and square, and he just couldn't believe that someone would ask him to do otherwise.

Eloisa sighed heavily. She turned and headed for the door, but then, all of a sudden, she fainted and collapsed on the floor.

"Oh!" Trixie cried. "She must be sick!"

Sparky rushed off to find a doctor. Trixie and Speed tried to help Eloisa up, but she could not stand up or even stay sitting on her own. Trixie covered her with a blanket. When she looked over at Speed, she saw a dark look on his face.

"Speed, why are you so angry?" Trixie whispered to him.

"You know I'm angry because of what this girl asked me to do!" Speed said.

"Well maybe she didn't realize that it was so wrong," Trixie said.

After the doctor checked to make sure Eloisa wasn't seriously injured, Speed and Trixie decided to drive her home. They wanted to be sure she made it back safely, without fainting again. Their drive took them to a small apartment building in a run-down part of the city.

Eloisa was still feeling too dizzy to walk, so Speed carried her up to her apartment. He was quickly intercepted by her brother, Hap Hazard, who grabbed her from Speed's arms.

"My sister!" Hap cried. "What happened?" Hap was about Speed's age and was dressed in a shabby racing uniform. He must have just come from driving practice.

"She came to see me and then she fainted," Speed said. "That's all."

"Fainted? Or maybe you and your friends beat her up so I'd have to take care of her and won't have time to be in the race," Hap said angrily.

"I would never hurt an innocent girl!" exclaimed Speed. He was getting angry again, shocked that anyone would accuse him of doing something so cruel.

"Get out of here!" shouted Hap.

Hap held his sister in his arms and whispered

to her. "Eloisa, speak to me. Tell me you'll be all right. I'll win that race and get the money to pay the doctors so they can make you well."

Hearing this, Trixie's heart started to sink. She felt terrible for Eloisa and Hap.

"Oh, Speed. She's really not well," Trixie said on the drive back to the hotel. "Maybe it wouldn't be so bad if Hap won this race."

"Hap can win," Speed said. "He'll just have to beat me first."

Part Two:
Nothing to Do with
Pineapples

Meanwhile, an angry criminal was trying to get some information. "You'd better tell me what you did with the king's jewel," he said to a man he had tied up to a chair.

The man whimpered but refused to say anything.

The criminal had a tiny little mustache and beady little eyes. "That diamond is bigger than my hand, and I must have it. I know you used the Pineapple Grand Prix to smuggle it into this country. Now tell me what car it's hidden in."

"I told you, it's not hidden in any car!" the man who was tied to the chair cried.

"Then where? Where is it?"

"It's in one of the pineapples."

"Which one?"

"I don't know. All the pineapples look the same to me."

"Don't you worry. I'll find it. I'll find that pineapple no matter what!" The criminal twirled his mustache and grinned. He was off to the race.

Part Three: Keep Your Eye on the Pineapple

The next day, Speed was deep in the middle of the Pineapple Grand Prix, trying to keep his mind off of his competitor Hap Hazard and his sick sister. As he drove, one by one, the other drivers were dropping out of the race. Speed had seen them on the roads behind him, but then they were gone. He didn't realize that a helicopter was flying low over the racecourse, and that the criminals were pulling pineapples out of cars using a rope and hook and breaking them open, trying to see if the king's jewel was hidden inside.

The criminals hadn't found the right pineapple yet.

Then they spied Hap Hazard driving through the Unknown Forest. A criminal was hidden in a tree. He threw a small ax at Hap's pineapple, catching it and sending it flying out of the car. Hap kept driving without noticing that it was missing from his passenger seat. But when the criminals cracked open the pineapple, they found only the sweet yellow fruit inside. No diamond.

The only driver left in the race with a pineapple was Speed. He, too, was driving through the Unknown Forest, a dark scary place

with low-hanging trees. He came across a fallen tree trunk and stopped the Mach 5 for a moment. Just then a flying ax came out of the trees. He ducked. Someone came to snatch his pineapple, but he grabbed it, hit the gas, and drove away.

I bet they're friends of Hap's, he thought. *They don't want me to finish the race, so they're trying to steal my pineapple! Hap shouldn't try to win the race this way. He should try to win fair and square.*

At the edge of the Unknown Forest, getting closer to the Valley of Destruction, Speed noticed a red car stopped in the road. A figure was standing beside it. It was Hap. "Stop, Speed Racer!" he shouted.

Speed screeched to a halt. "What do you want?" he said. "We're in the middle of a race."

"My pineapple," Hap said. "One of your men took it from me."

"What are you talking about?" Speed retorted.

"Your men tried to take my pineapple from me in the forest!"

"So you still have your pineapple, then, do you?" Hap said. Suddenly he leaped forward, grabbed Speed's pineapple from his front seat, and took off in his red race car!

Speed had no choice but to follow. He sure couldn't win the race without his pineapple.

The chase led them through the deepest bowels of the Valley of Destruction. The roads weren't even roads here. They cut through rocks and craters. Chasms opened up in the middle of the path. Avalanches of rock rained down and caused Hap and Speed to take detours, ignoring the map completely just to get through it.

Speed was determined to catch up to Hap and grab his pineapple back. He had the perfect opportunity when the two racers reached a swamp.

Hap made a sharp turn, and his car got stuck

in a deep patch of mud. The mud started pooling up around his tires, until soon his car was buried in it. A mud slide! Speed used the special controls in the Mach 5 to keep himself afloat, but he saw Hap's red car drifting in the swamp, coming very close to the edge of a cliff.

Speed could just jump over, grab his pineapple, and get back in the race. He'd win the race for sure with Hap stuck in the mud.

But he couldn't just leave Hap there. Hap's car could topple over, and he'd drown in mud. Speed had to help him.

"Hang on, Hap!" he cried. "Stay right there!" He connected a cable to the Mach 5 and waded into the mud to secure the other end to Hap's car. Then, with the force of the Mach 5's engine and the grip of his belt tires, he was able to pull Hap's race car out of the mud slide.

"Okay, Hap, I got you out. You can go on with the race," Speed said. He approached Hap's window to see if he was okay, and also to get his pineapple back.

"I owe you my life, Speed," Hap said. "I will not forget. But I am still going to try to beat you in this race! And I am not going to give this pineapple back."

"Yes, you are, Hap. You know that pineapple's mine. You will give it back."

"I will not!"

"You will."

A plane sounded overhead.

"What's that?" Speed cried.

Men leaped out of the plane with parachutes. When they hit ground, they went immediately for the one remaining pineapple. Speed and Hap fought them off, running with the pineapple and throwing it between them, but when Speed saw an opening and had the pineapple safely in his hands, he went for it. He leaped into the Mach 5 and took off, back into the race. Out of the corner of his eye, he saw the men stop running. Hap jumped into his car and followed.

I wonder why someone wants this pineapple so badly, Speed thought. *Oh well. I'm not letting go of it until I win this race.*

Part Four:
A Prize of Pineapples

Speed and Hap drove neck and neck all the way to the finish, but Speed was the one to cross the finish line first. He leaped out of his car, cheering wildly. He had won the Pineapple Grand

Prix, fair and square! He tried not to look over at Hap, who was staring sullenly at his steering wheel, utterly depressed that he had lost. He put his head in his hands.

Little did Speed know that as he was celebrating, his pineapple was not sitting safely in the front seat of his car as he'd left it. Chim Chim had snuck into the Mach 5 and stolen the pineapple, putting it in Hap's car instead. Trixie, feeling bad for Hap and his sister, had asked Chim Chim to help Hap win.

"Now, ladies and gentlemen," the announcer was saying to the crowd, "we must check to make sure that the winner still has the pineapple in his possession. Speed, will you please show us your pineapple?"

Speed smiled and went over to get his pineapple, but it was gone!

The racing officials crowded around the Mach 5. "I can't understand," Speed said. "I just had it. I don't know where it went."

"If you don't have your pineapple, you're disqualified," the announcer said. "Mr. Hazard, do you have your pineapple?"

"No, I am sorry, I do not," Hap said. Then he happened to look at his passenger seat and there, as if by magic, was a pineapple. "I cannot believe it!" he cried. "I do have a pineapple! I do!"

"Hap Hazard is the winner of the Pineapple Grand Prix!" the announcer said. The crowd cheered. Hap held up the pineapple, but suddenly, from out of the crowd, a man with a thin mustache and beady eyes ran over to him. He tackled Hap, snatched the pineapple, and made a run for it. Speed intercepted him and grabbed for the pineapple. They struggled, and the pineapple flew onto the ground at their feet.

It smashed open. There was nothing inside but fruit.

The announcer went on with the winning announcements. "Hap Hazard has won ten thousand dollars, and also a ten-year supply of pineapples!" he cried.

"Please," Hap said, ecstatic at having won, "please share the pineapples with the fans." His sister stood at his side, beaming, as the pineapples rained down onto the racetrack. Everyone in the crowd ran out to grab one.

The man with the mustache howled. "The king's jewel must be in one of those pineapples," he said. He ran for the pile. "Out of the way, brats," he yelled to some kids. Spritle and Chim Chim were among them. The man with the mustache and his men started hacking through the pineapples, looking for the jewel.

Suddenly Chim Chim bit into something hard. He spat it out: a giant, gleaming diamond.

"The king's jewel!" the criminal yelled loudly. Just as he said that, a police officer grabbed it and looked up.

"Looking for this?" the officer said.

Speed stood off to the side, watching as the criminal was arrested by the police. Now he understood why those men were trying to steal his pineapple during the race.

Trixie approached him. "I have a confession to make, Speed," she said. "You can blame me for Hap winning the Grand Prix. I told Chim Chim to give him the pineapple. I just wanted him to win, Speed. So he could take care of his sister. Are you mad?"

Speed didn't answer.

"Speed? Speed? Are you mad? What are you looking at?"

"That," Speed said. He wasn't mad at all. He watched Hap and his sister hug each other, now knowing they had the money to take care of her hospital bills. "I know why you did it, Trixie, and it's for the best. I don't mind not winning this time." He gave Trixie a smile. "You know what I want right about now?"

"What?"

"A pineapple!" he exclaimed. And they ran over to grab one before Spritle and Chim Chim ate them all.

SPEED RACER™
THE NEXT GENERATION

Racing to DVD
May 2008

Classic Speed Racer DVDs
Also Available!